READ AND SHARE®
5-MINUTE BIBLE
BIBLE
STORIES

Stories Retold by
Gwen Ellis

Illustrated by Steve Smallman

A Division of Thomas Nelson Publishers

NASHVILLE   DALLAS   MEXICO CITY   RIO DE JANEIRO

Read and Share® 5-Minute Bible Stories
© 2015 by Thomas Nelson

Published in Nashville, Tennessee, by Tommy Nelson. Tommy Nelson is an imprint of Thomas
Nelson. Thomas Nelson is a registered trademark of HarperCollins Christian Publishing, Inc.

Stories retold by Gwen Ellis
Illustrated by Steve Smallman

Tommy Nelson titles may be purchased in bulk for educational, business, fund-raising, or sales
promotional use. For information, please e-mail SpecialMarkets@ThomasNelson.com.

Stories based on the INTERNATIONAL CHILDREN'S BIBLE®. © 1986,
1988, 1999 by Thomas Nelson, Inc. All rights reserved.

ISBN-13: 978-0-7180-3658-4

Library of Congress Cataloging-in-Publication Data is on file.

Printed in China

15 16 17 18 19 TIMS 5 4 3 2 1

Mfr.: TIMS / Shenzhen, China / July 2015 / PO # 9342882

Contents

New Testament Stories

Old Testament

The First Day

Genesis 1:1–5

In the beginning God made heaven and earth. At first it was empty and dark. But God gathered up the light and called it *day*.

Then He gathered up the darkness and called it *night*. God was watching over everything.

What do you think God did next?

The Second Day

Genesis 1:6–8

On day two God divided the air from the water. He put some water above the air and some below it. He named the air *sky*.

The next day God made something many children like, especially in the summer. Can you guess what it is?

The Third Day

Genesis 1:9–13

On day three God was busy. He made puddles and oceans and lakes and waterfalls and rivers. He made the dry ground too.

Next He made plants. He made so many different kinds of trees, flowers, and bushes that no one could count them all. God said His work was good.

**Wow! God made so much on that day.
But can you guess what was missing?**

The Fourth Day

Genesis 1:14–19

On day four God put the sun in the sky to warm the earth. He saw that the night was very dark, so God put the moon and the stars in the sky.

Then God made spring, summer, fall, and winter. All that He made was good.

**Next God made flippy, flappy fun things.
Let's see what they were.**

The Fifth Day

Genesis 1:20–23

On day five God made starfishes, octopuses, whales, and turtles. He made fast little fish for rivers and slippery big fish for the ocean.

He made big birds like eagles to soar in the sky and zippy little birds like hummingbirds. He made birds in all shapes, sizes, and colors.

Which bird do you think is the prettiest?
Which is the strongest?

The Sixth Day

Genesis 1:24–31

On day six God made the animals—
puppies, cows, horses, kitties, bears,
lizards, mice, worms, and lots more.
Everything was good.

But something was still missing. There were no people. So God made some. And when He made them, He made them like Himself. He made them so they could be friends with Him.

Where do you think the first people lived?

Adam and Eve

Genesis 2:1–5, 15–22; 3:20

God named the first man Adam. God put Adam in a beautiful garden. He gave him all the animals. He gave him all the fish and the birds too.

Then God gave Adam one more thing.
God made a woman to be Adam's wife.
Adam named his wife Eve. On day seven
God rested from all His work.

**Uh-oh. Something bad was about to happen
on the earth.**

The Sneaky Snake

Genesis 2:16–17; 3:1–6

God gave Adam and Eve one rule. "Eat anything you like except the fruit from the tree in the middle of the garden."

A sneaky old snake came to Eve. "Eat it, then you'll know everything, just like God." So Eve ate the fruit and gave some to Adam. And he ate it too.

When we disobey God, it's called *sin*. There are always consequences when we disobey.

Out of the Garden

Genesis 3:8–24

One evening God came to visit Adam and Eve. But they were hiding. When God found them, He asked, "What have you done?" Adam told God everything. God was sad.

Because they had disobeyed God, Adam and Eve had to leave the beautiful garden. When they were outside of the garden, Adam and Eve had to work very hard to grow food.

It makes God very sad when we disobey. It makes our parents sad too.

Noah

Genesis 6

Many years later there were lots of people on the earth, but most of them were bad. One man—Noah—was good. He obeyed God. "I want you to build a boat," God told Noah.

Noah started right away. People laughed at Noah because they lived in a desert and there was no water for his boat. Noah just went on building the boat.

Do you think it is easy to obey when everyone is laughing at you?

The Big Boat

Genesis 7:1–15

When the boat was finished, God told Noah and his family to go into the boat. In went his sons Shem, Ham, and Japheth. In went their wives and Mrs. Noah.

"Now bring two of every animal," God told Noah. Noah did exactly what God told him to do. And God watched over him.

Something very wet was about to happen outside.

Inside the Boat

Genesis 7:16–24

When the last animal climbed into the boat, God shut the door. *Plip! Plop! Plip!* It began to rain. It rained so much, the water was over the meadows. It rained so much, it covered the towns. It rained so much, it even covered the mountains.

But inside the boat, everyone was safe.

How many days do you think it rained?

The Dove

Genesis 7:12; 8:1–19

After 40 days and 40 nights, the rain stopped, but it still wasn't time to get off the boat. Water was everywhere. One day Noah let a little dove fly out to see what was happening on the earth.

It brought a green leaf back. Hooray! The plants were growing again! It was almost time to come out!

What do you think everyone did when Noah opened the door of the boat?

The Rainbow

Genesis 8:18–22; 9:1–17

When everyone was out of the boat, Noah built an altar. He thanked God for keeping them safe. Then something wonderful happened!

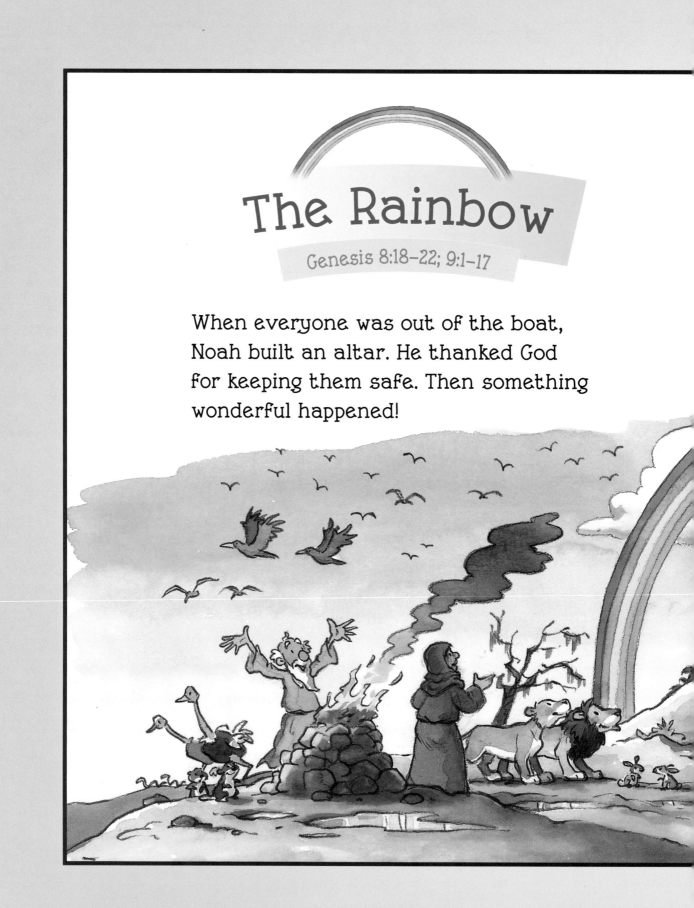

God put a beautiful rainbow in the sky and made Noah a promise. "It will never flood over the whole earth like that again," God said. When God makes a promise, He keeps it.

All God's promises are in the Bible. Isn't it wonderful to think of all He has promised us?

Abram

Genesis 12:1–3; 15:5; 22:17

God picked Abram to be the father of a very important family. One day in the future, Jesus would come from this family.

God told Abram, "I will make you famous. Your children and grandchildren will be as many as the stars. They will be as many as the grains of sand on the beach. You won't be able to count them."

Wow! That's a wonderful promise. How do you think Abram felt?

Promised Land

Genesis 12:1–9

God told Abram to move to a new place. Abram had no map. God said, "I will show you where to go." Abram started out walking. He took his wife, nephew, and servants with him.

When Abram and his family got to a land called Canaan, God said, "This is your new home. I am giving it to you and to everyone who will ever be in your family."

If your parents said, "We're going on a trip, but we can't tell you where," would you trust them to take you to a good place?

Abraham's Visitors

Genesis 17:1–8; 18:1–8

When Abram was 99 years old, God changed his name to Abraham. His new name showed that he belonged to God. Not long after that, three men came by Abraham's tent, and he invited them to lunch.

"Quick! Bake some bread," Abraham told his wife. Then Abraham hurried to get some meat cooked. When the food was ready, Abraham brought it to his visitors. The men sat down to eat.

Abraham didn't know it, but his visitors were from heaven.

Sarah Laughs

Genesis 18:9–16

When one of the visitors finished eating, he said, "Where is your wife, Sarah?" "She's over there in the tent," Abraham said. "Next year Sarah will have a baby," the visitor said.

Sarah heard and laughed. She couldn't believe it. *I'm too old to have a baby,* she thought. *Abraham is too old too.*

What if your great-grandmother had a baby? Sarah was that old. Let's see how God keeps His promises.

Baby Isaac

Genesis 21:1–7

In about a year Sarah had a baby boy, just like God had promised. Abraham named the baby Isaac. Isaac means "laughter."

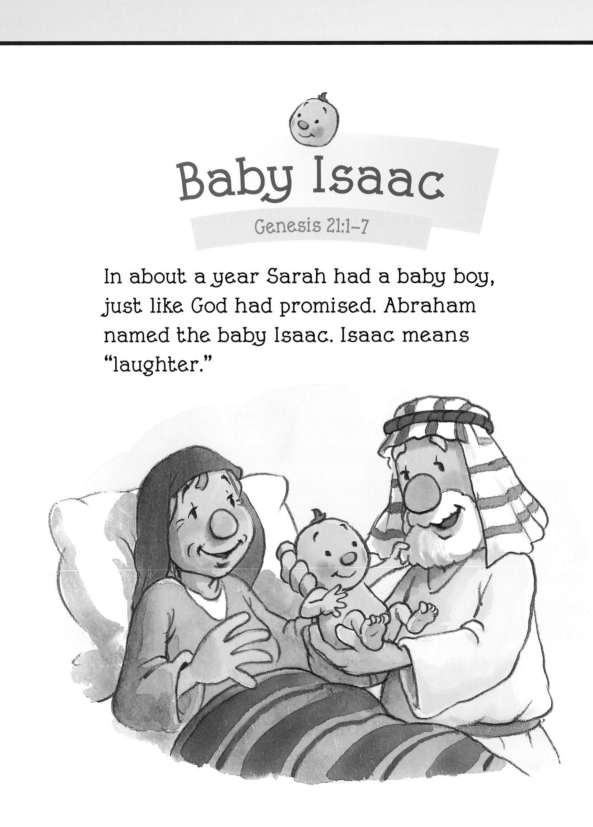

Sarah was so happy with her baby boy.
She said, "God has made me laugh.
Everyone who hears about this will
laugh with me."

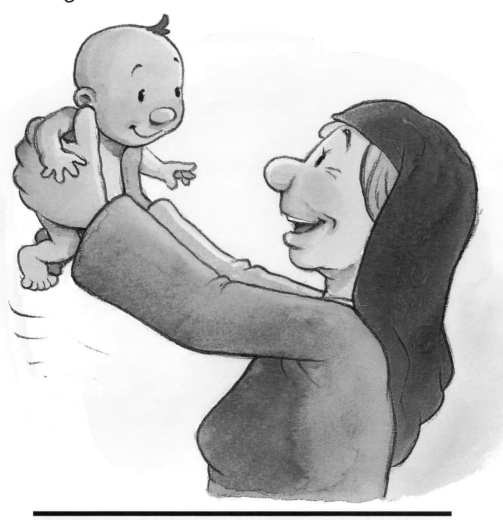

**God can do anything, but sometimes it takes a while
to see the answer. What would you like to ask Him
to do for you?**

A Mean King

Exodus 1:8–14

Years later a mean king made the Israelites his slaves. The slave masters were mean too. They made the Israelites work harder and harder to make bricks and do other things for the king.

"There are too many Israelites, and they are too strong," said the king. So he thought up an awful thing to do.

Why do you think the king was mean to the Israelites?

A Baby Boy

Exodus 1:22–2:2

That mean old king said, "Every time an Israelite baby boy is born, you must throw him into the river." That was terrible!

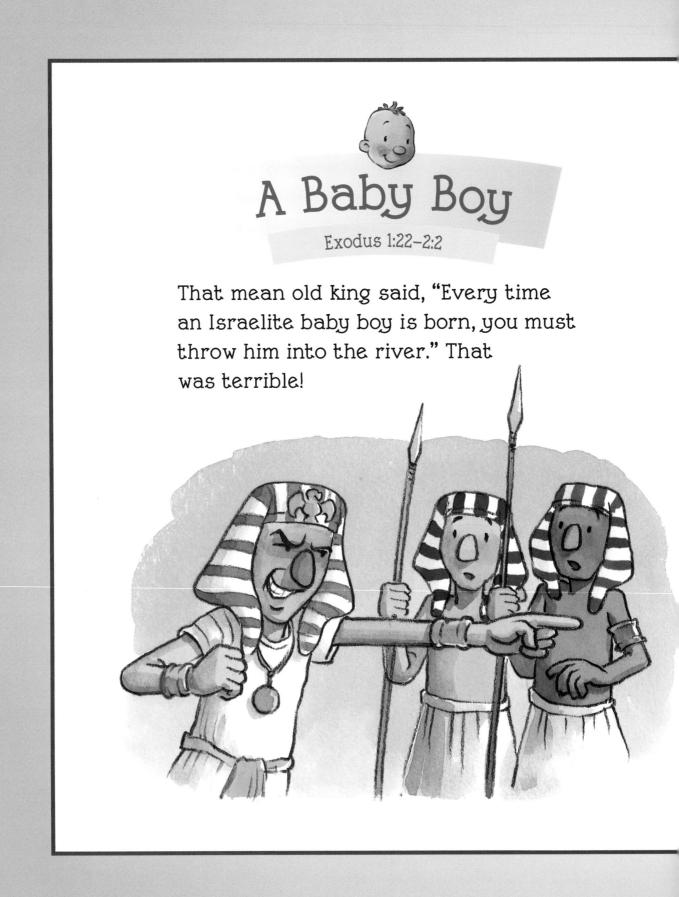

One day an Israelite woman had a beautiful baby boy. She decided to hide her baby from the evil king and his helpers. It was a good choice.

When we make the right choice, God always helps us. Let's see what happened next.

The Good Sister

Exodus 2:3–4

After a while the baby's mother couldn't hide him anymore. So she got a basket and fixed it so the water could not get inside.

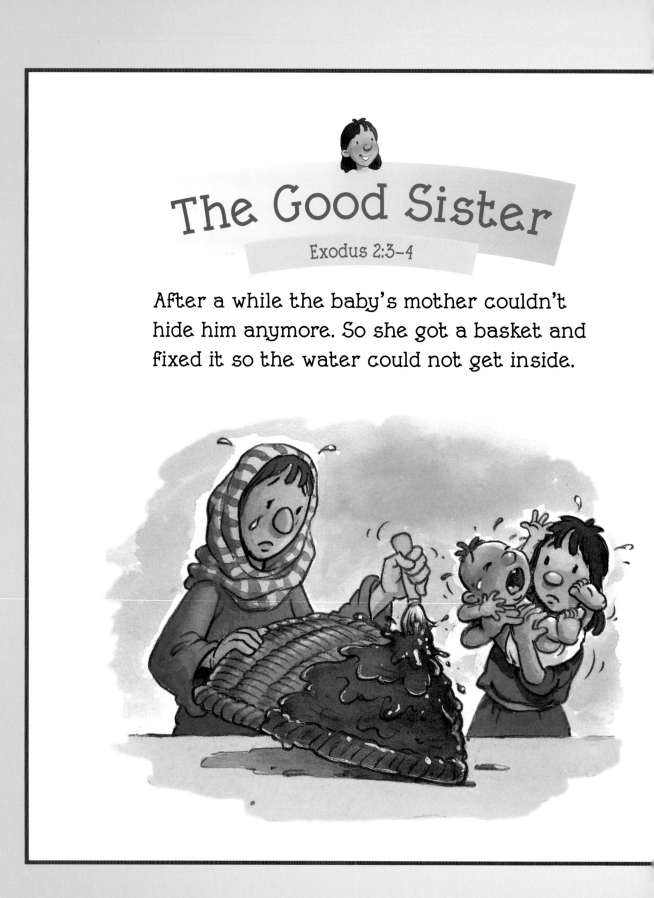

Then she put the baby into the basket and put the basket into the river. The baby's big sister, Miriam, stayed close by to see what would happen.

Miriam must have been very frightened. What do you think she said when she prayed for her little brother?

A Princess
Finds Moses

Exodus 2:5–10

God was watching over the baby. When the princess came to the river to take a bath, she saw the basket. "Go get that basket," she told her servant.

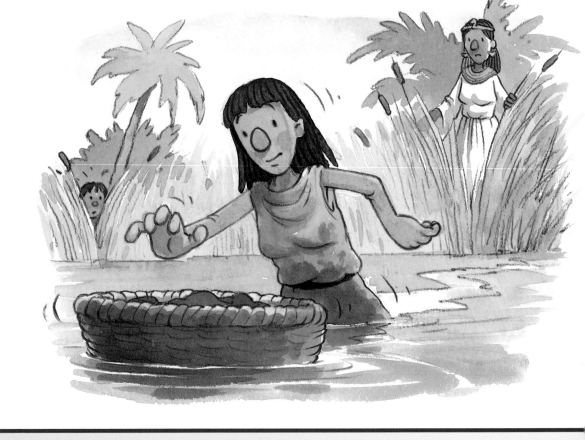

The princess looked inside the basket. Just then the baby cried, and she felt sorry for him. The princess decided to keep him as her son. She named him Moses.

This was exciting! Moses was going to be a prince of Egypt. But something even better was about to happen.

Moses' Real Mother Helps

Exodus 2:7–10

Miriam was still watching. Even though she was frightened, she stepped out and asked, "Do you need someone to take care of the baby?" The princess smiled. "Why, yes," she replied.

Miriam ran home and got her mother—
Moses' own mother—to take care of
him. God saved Baby Moses and gave
him back to his mother for a long time.

Many exciting things were going to happen
to Moses when he grew up. Let's read on.

Moses Runs Away

Exodus 2:11–3:3

After a while Moses went to the palace to live. When he was grown up, Moses did something very bad. He killed another man.

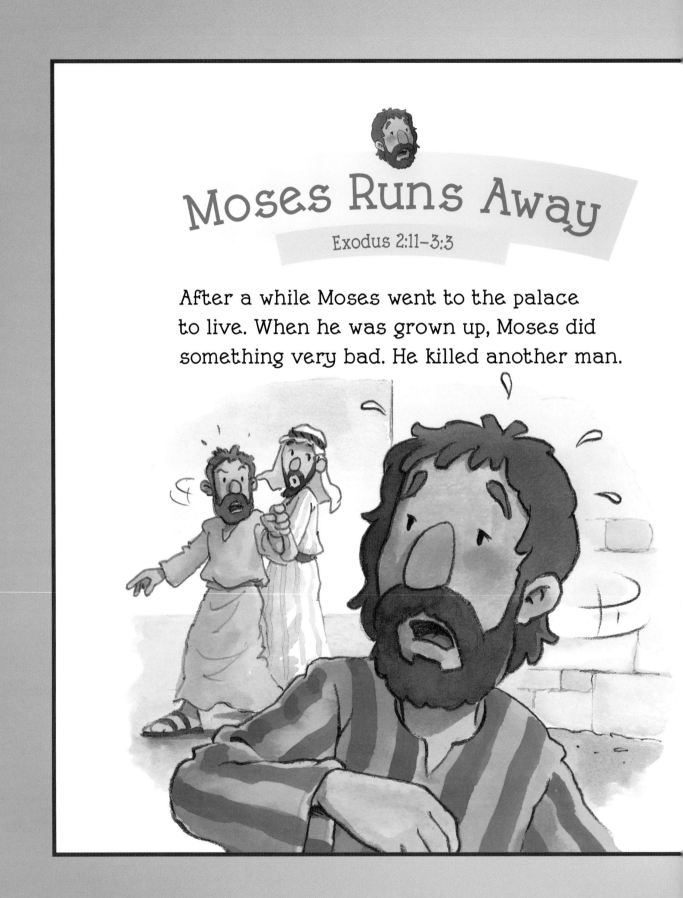

Moses ran away to live in the desert. He married a lady named Zipporah. Her father's name was Jethro. One day when Moses was out with the sheep, he saw a bush in the desert. It was on fire, but it didn't burn up.

What was going on? Why didn't the bush burn up?

Strange Fire

Exodus 3:4–12

Moses went to look at this strange fire. God spoke to Moses from the fire. "Don't come any closer. Take off your sandals. You are on holy ground." Moses was scared. He covered his face. "Go, bring My people out of Egypt," God said.

"I can't do that," Moses said. But God promised to help Moses lead the people.

Whenever God asks us to do hard things, He will help us. Let's see how He helped Moses.

Moses Goes Home

Exodus 4:14–5:1

Moses went home to Egypt to talk to the Israelites about being free. God sent Moses' brother Aaron to help him.

The Israelites fell right down on their knees and thanked God for remembering them. Then it was time for Moses to go see the mean king. Moses took Aaron with him.

Oh my! Moses had to ask the king to let all those people go free. What do you think the king said?

The King Says No!

Exodus 5:1–9

Moses walked right up to the king and said, "God says, 'Let My people go!'" The king said, "I don't know your God. Why should I obey Him? These people have work to do. They cannot leave."

Then the king made the people work even harder. What a mean man! This made the Israelite leaders angry with Moses.

Do you think Moses made a mistake?

A Mistake?

Exodus 5:19–6:9

The Israelite leaders were angry. They thought Moses had surely made a big mistake. "You made the king hate us," they said.

Moses talked to God. "Lord, why have You brought this trouble on the people? Is this why You sent me here?" God answered, "You will see what I will do to the king."

Sometimes even when we do good, things get worse for a while. This is when we need to remember that God can see ahead.

The Walking-Stick Miracle

Exodus 7:8–13

God sent Moses and Aaron back to the king. "Let God's people go," Moses said. "Do a miracle," said the king. Aaron threw down his walking stick, and it became a snake.

The king's magicians threw down their sticks, and they became snakes too. But Aaron's snake swallowed them all. God's power was the strongest. Still the king was so evil and his heart was so hard that he said, "No, your people cannot leave."

This is just getting harder and harder. How will God rescue His people?

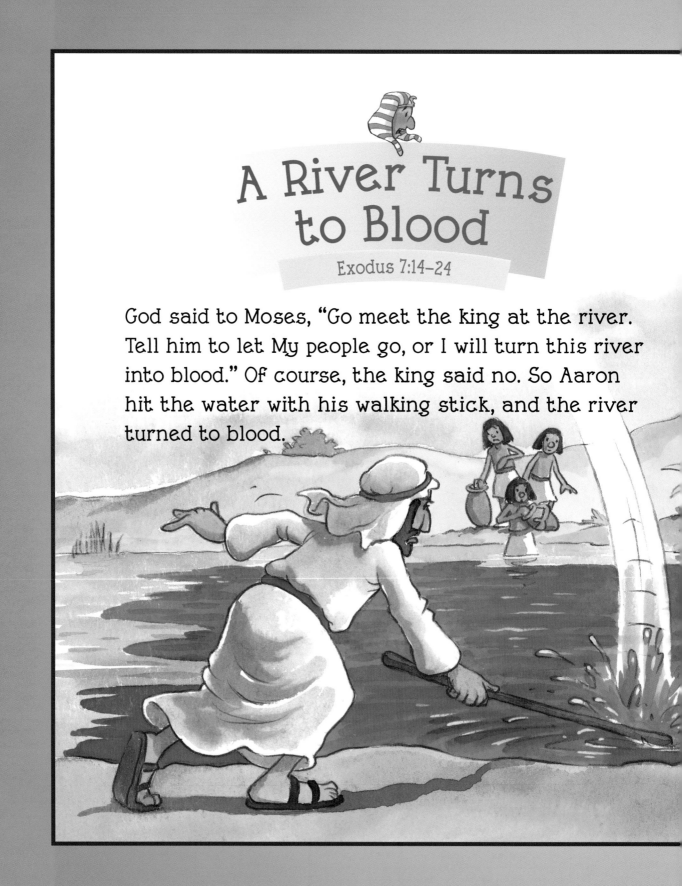

A River Turns to Blood

Exodus 7:14–24

God said to Moses, "Go meet the king at the river. Tell him to let My people go, or I will turn this river into blood." Of course, the king said no. So Aaron hit the water with his walking stick, and the river turned to blood.

It smelled awful, and there was no water for the people to drink.

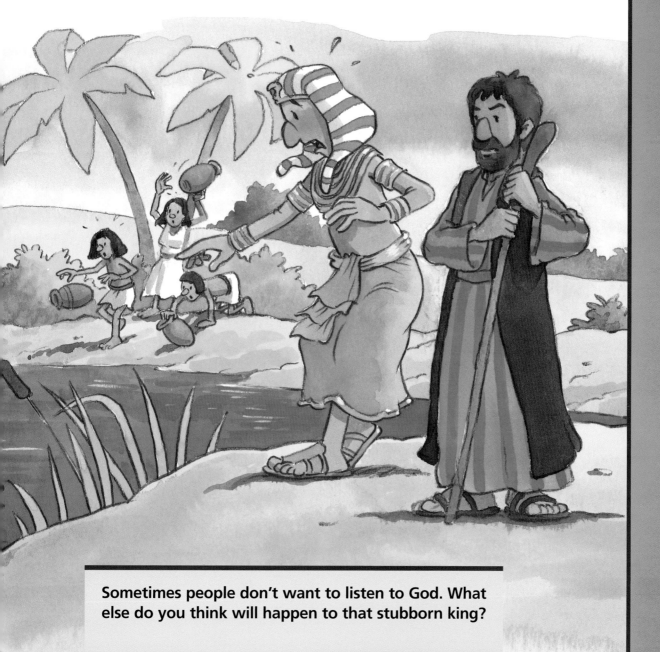

Sometimes people don't want to listen to God. What else do you think will happen to that stubborn king?

Frogs, Frogs, Frogs

Exodus 7:25–8:15

After seven days Moses went back to the king. "Let God's people go," said Moses. "No," said the king.

This time God sent frogs. Not just one or two, but more than anyone could count! The frogs went in the houses, in the beds, in the food, and in the ovens. The frogs were icky, and they were everywhere.

God meant business. How much worse do you think it will get before the king says yes?

Gnats, Flies, and Boils

Exodus 8:16–9:12

Every time the king said no, things just went from bad to worse in Egypt. God sent little bitty gnats that crawled all over the people.

Next He sent millions of flies. They were everywhere. Cows got sick and died. Then people got sick with big sores called *boils*. But the king still said no each time.

That king sure was stubborn! Can you guess what awful thing came next?

Hail, Locusts, and Darkness

Exodus 9:13–10:29

Next God sent a storm. Big chunks of ice called *hail* pounded every plant into the ground. Then hungry grasshoppers called *locusts* blew in with the wind. There were so many of them, the people couldn't see the ground. The grasshoppers ate all the food.

Then God sent darkness right in the middle of the day. The Egyptians couldn't see anything. But the king still said no.

Why do you think the king kept saying no?

Standing-Up Dinner

Exodus 11:1–12:28

God told His people to fix a dinner of roast lamb and to eat dinner standing up with all their clothes on.

He told them to have their walking sticks in their hands. God knew the king would soon change his mind, and His people needed to be ready to go.

On this night the children got to stay up late and eat dinner with their parents.
Tell what you think happened next.

Something Awful

Exodus 12:29–51

At midnight because the king was so stubborn, something awful happened in Egypt. All the oldest boys, cows, horses, and other animals died. But not one of God's people or their animals died.

Finally the king said, "Take everything you have and leave Egypt." God's people were free at last!

God doesn't want bad things to happen to people, but He had to make the king listen.

Cloud and Fire

Exodus 13:21–22

When God's people left Egypt, they marched out into the desert. God did something very special to help them. He sent a tall cloud to guide them during the day.

It was very dark in the desert at night. So God changed the cloud to fire. It was like a giant night-light. Now God's people could travel some during the day and some at night.

God loved His people. He was taking care of them just like He takes care of us.

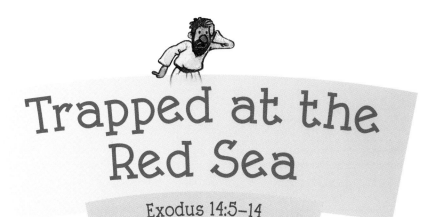

Trapped at the Red Sea

Exodus 14:5–14

Back in Egypt the king changed his mind.
He sent his army after the Israelites to
bring them back. Closer and closer the
army of horses and chariots came.

God's people stood right by the Red Sea.
There was no way across the water. The
king's soldiers were behind them, and
the sea was in front of them. It looked as
if they were trapped, but they weren't.

**How do you think God's people felt at that moment?
Sad? Scared? Hopeful?**

A Dry Path

Exodus 14:15–31

Just then God moved the tall cloud behind His people to hide them from the enemy. The Egyptians couldn't see anything. The cloud made it dark for them. But it gave light to God's people on the other side of the cloud.

Then Moses raised his hand over the sea. All night God pushed back the sea with a strong wind. And the water split to make a dry path to the other side. The Israelites safely reached the other side. But when the Egyptian army tried to use the same path, the water came back together and covered the soldiers. And that was the end of the king's army.

Can you imagine what it was like to walk on a path in the middle of the sea?

Food and Water

Exodus 15:22–17:7

God led His people through the desert. God loved them. He made sure they had plenty of food and water. He gave them a strange, white food called *manna*. It came from the sky and was very good for them, but the people whined and whined.

Once God even made water come out of
a rock so they would have fresh water to
drink. The people were happy to have water.
They stopped whining for a little while.

**God wants us to be thankful. What are you
thankful for? What should you tell God?**

Ten Commandments

Exodus 20:2–17; 24:12–18

One day God called Moses up to the top of a mountain to have a talk.

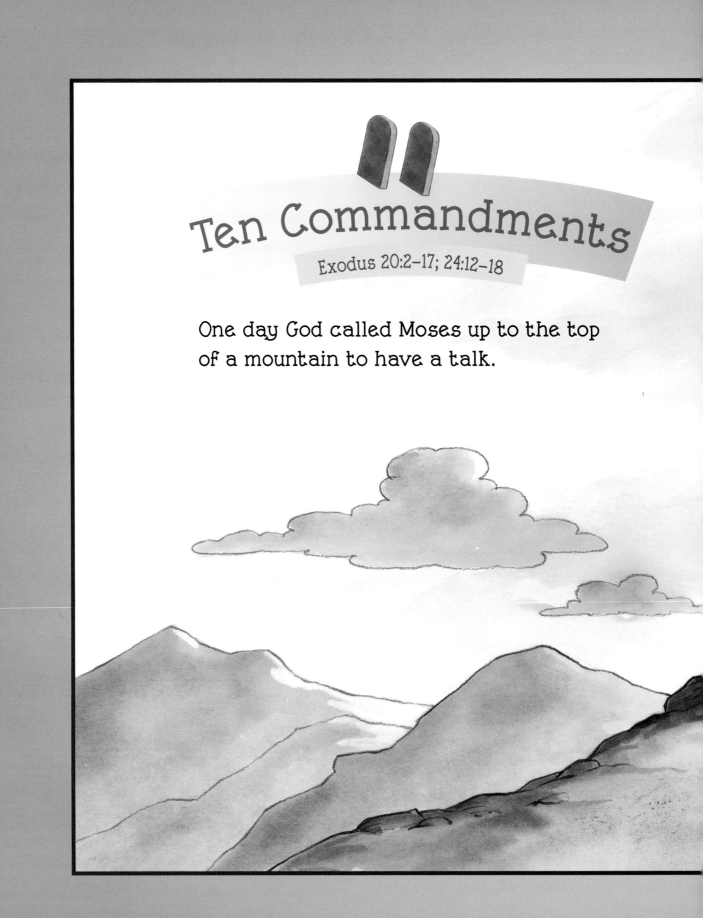

God gave Moses many rules to help His people know how to live. God wrote the rules on stone with His finger. We call these rules *The Ten Commandments*.

God gives us rules to keep us safe. Rules help us live happy lives. Moms and dads have rules too. Can you name one?

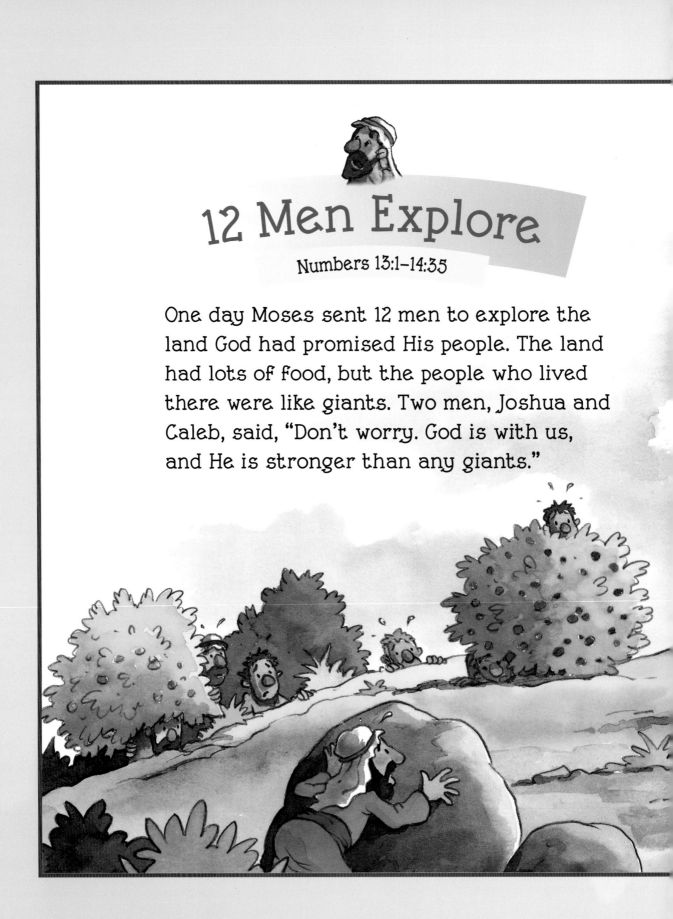

12 Men Explore

Numbers 13:1–14:35

One day Moses sent 12 men to explore the land God had promised His people. The land had lots of food, but the people who lived there were like giants. Two men, Joshua and Caleb, said, "Don't worry. God is with us, and He is stronger than any giants."

But the other men were afraid and said, "We can't go into the land." God was not happy with His people. They did not trust Him. So God's people had to wander around in the desert 40 more years.

God wants us to believe His Word.
Of the 12 men who explored the new land, which two trusted God?

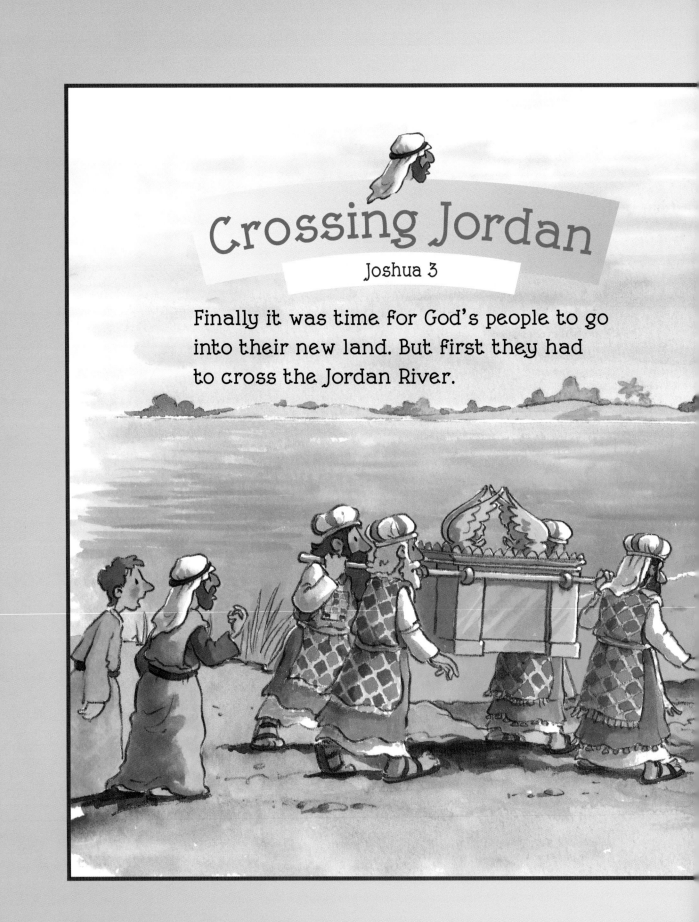

Crossing Jordan

Joshua 3

Finally it was time for God's people to go into their new land. But first they had to cross the Jordan River.

There were no bridges or boats. God told the priests to carry the Holy Box and walk into the water. When they did, God made a dry path, and His people walked across to the other side of the river.

What do you think other people thought when they heard what God did for His people?

The Walls of Jericho

Joshua 6

The first city they came to was Jericho. It had huge walls and gates and guards everywhere. God said, "March around Jericho every day for six days. Seven priests with trumpets must march at the front."

"On the seventh day, march around seven times. Then have the priests blow one long blast on their trumpets. The people must shout and the walls will fall down." The people obeyed and down came those walls.

Sometimes God asks us to do things we don't understand. We just need to obey.

Ruth and Naomi

Ruth 1

Ruth and Naomi were widows. That means their husbands had died. Ruth had been married to Naomi's son. One day Naomi decided to go back to the land from which her family had come.

Ruth decided to go with her. Naomi thought Ruth might miss her family and friends. She told Ruth not to come with her. But Ruth said, "Don't ask me to leave you!" And so they went together.

Ruth didn't know where she was going, and she didn't know the big surprise waiting for her. Try to guess what it was.

Ruth Gathers Grain

Ruth 2

Ruth and Naomi were very poor. They didn't have enough to eat. Naomi was too old to work, so Ruth went out to a rich man's field to gather leftover grain for food. The rich man saw her. She was a beautiful young woman. "Stay here and work in my field," he told her.

Ruth was taking care of Naomi, and God was taking care of them both. But God wasn't finished with His surprise yet. What will it be?

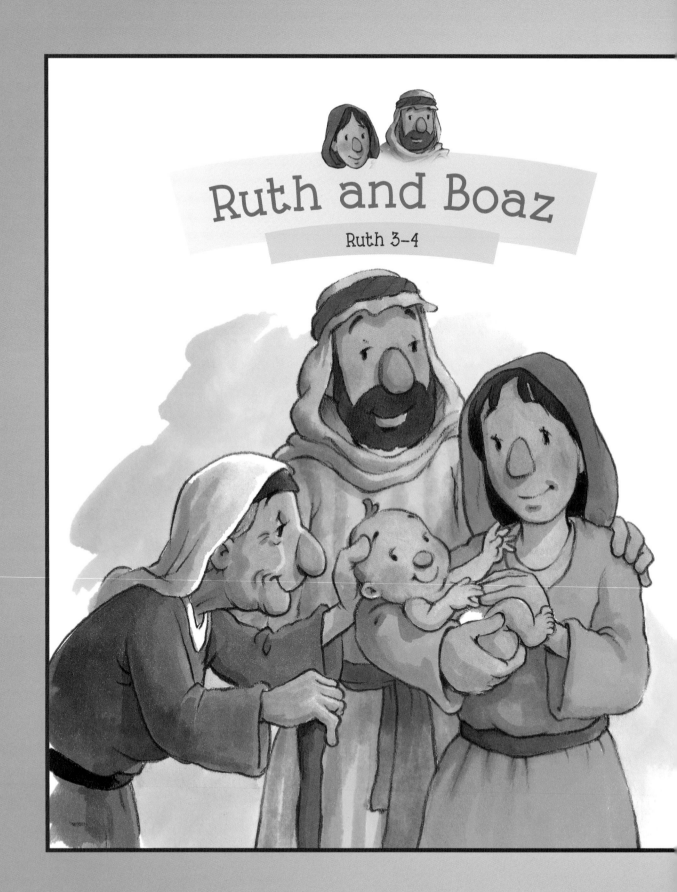

Ruth and Boaz

Ruth 3–4

Naomi decided Boaz would be a good husband for Ruth. She told Ruth what she should do to see if Boaz wanted to marry her. Ruth did exactly what Naomi said. Boaz liked Ruth and wanted to marry her. So they were married and had a little boy. That made all of them happy.

God's surprises are always very special if we can just wait for His time to give them to us. Tell about a surprise you've had.

The Youngest Son

1 Samuel 16:1–13

God sent Samuel to the house of a man named Jesse to choose a new king. When Samuel looked at seven of Jesse's sons, God said to him, "Don't look at how tall or handsome they are."

"Are these all of your sons?" Samuel asked. Jesse said, "My youngest son is taking care of the sheep. His name is David." God said to Samuel, "David is the one I've chosen."

God doesn't care if you are tall or short or have blue eyes or brown. He just wants you to have a heart that loves Him.

David and the Giant

1 Samuel 17:1–24

God's Holy Spirit came to be with David. It made him brave and strong. One day Jesse told David to go check on his brothers who were soldiers. When David got to the battlefield, he found the soldiers were all afraid of a giant named Goliath. Goliath liked to yell at the soldiers and scare them. He wanted to hurt them.

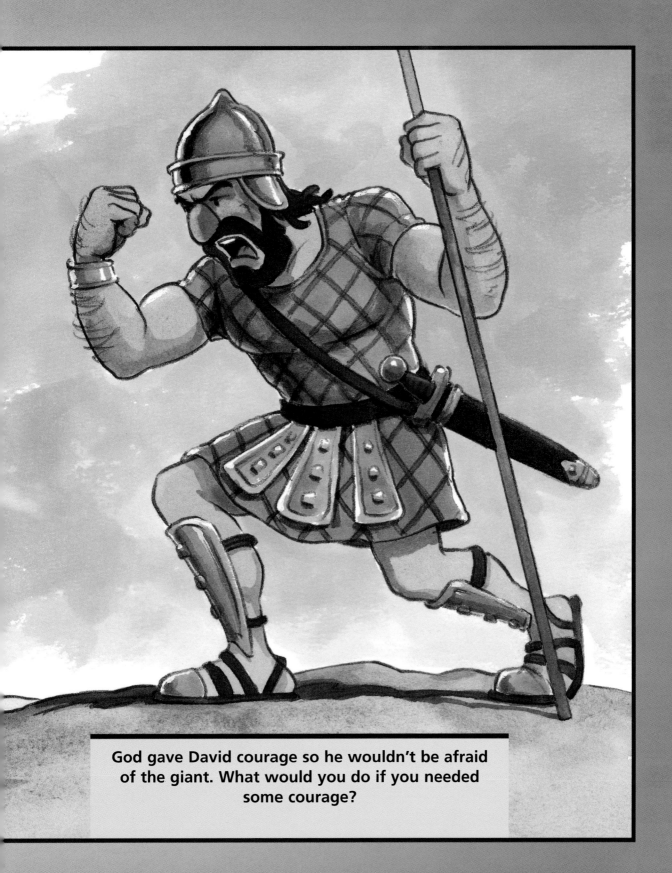

God gave David courage so he wouldn't be afraid of the giant. What would you do if you needed some courage?

Down Goes the Giant

1 Samuel 17:25–58

David wasn't afraid of Goliath. He gathered five smooth small stones and put them in his pouch. Then with his slingshot in one hand, David went to meet Goliath.

The giant laughed when he saw that David was just a boy. But David shot a stone from the slingshot. It hit Goliath in the head and killed him.

David was brave, and he trusted God. God will help us in scary times if we just ask Him.

Captured!

2 Kings 24:18–25:21; 2 Chronicles 36:15–23

Over and over God had warned His people not to worship idols. But they kept right on doing what God had told them not to do. So finally God let an enemy capture His people and take them from the land He'd given them. They were taken far away to a place called Babylon. It was a sad day.

God wants us to do what is right, and He is very patient. But if we continue to do wrong, we will have to suffer the consequences.

Beautiful Queen Esther

Esther 1–3

Years later the Persian kingdom defeated Babylon. But God's people were still living in the land of Babylon. One of them was a young woman named Esther.

The king of Persia wanted a beautiful young woman to be his queen. He picked Esther. Soon afterward one of the king's men decided to get rid of all God's people in the kingdom. Since Esther was one of them, it meant he would get rid of her too.

It must have been a very scary time for Esther.
What do you think she did?

Esther Saves Her People

Esther 4–9

Esther knew it was up to her to save her people. She also knew that if she visited the king and he got angry, she wouldn't be queen anymore. The king could even have her killed. What should she do?

Esther decided to go to the king anyway.
When she went, the king granted her wish
that her people would be allowed to live.

Esther was very brave. She did what God wanted
her to do, and because she was brave, she
saved her people. Yea, Esther!

Jonah Runs Away

Jonah 1:1–3

"Go to Nineveh," God told a man named Jonah. "Tell them to stop their evil ways." Jonah got up, but he didn't go to Nineveh. He didn't like the people of that city, so he ran away.

Jonah went to the seashore. He got on a ship going the opposite direction from Nineveh. God saw what Jonah was doing.

God always sees what we are doing. He wants us to make good choices.

A Big Storm!

Jonah 1:4–6

Jonah sailed away on the ship. When the ship was at sea, God sent a big storm. Waves pounded the ship. The sailors were very frightened of the storm.

The captain went down into the bottom
of the ship and found Jonah sleeping.
"Get up and pray to your God too," he
said. "Maybe your God will save us!"

**The captain and everyone prayed.
They knew they needed help from somebody
bigger than themselves.**

Jonah Goes Overboard

Jonah 1:7–16

"Somebody has done something to cause this storm. Let's find out who it is," the sailors said. They decided the storm was Jonah's fault. "You're right. I ran away from God," Jonah told them. "Throw me into the sea. Then it will calm down."

So the sailors tossed Jonah overboard. As soon as Jonah was in the water, the sea became calm.

You might think that would be the end of Jonah, but it wasn't!

Inside a Big Fish!

Jonah 1:17–2:9

Down, down into the swirling water went Jonah. Then *gulp!* Something swallowed him. Jonah was in the stomach of a big fish. God left him there to learn something important. It took three days and three nights.

Then Jonah prayed to God for help. He decided to do what God had told him to do.

It took a while for Jonah to catch on that he needed to obey God. Now, how was he going to get out of that fish?

Jonah Obeys God

Jonah 2:10–3:10

God had a plan. He spoke to that fish.
It swam up close to the beach and spit
Jonah out of its stomach onto dry land.

Right away God said to Jonah, "Get up and go to the great city of Nineveh. Say what I tell you to say." This time Jonah didn't argue. He obeyed. He jumped up and went straight to Nineveh.

Every time we disobey, we get in trouble. What would be a better choice?

New Testament

An Angel's Message

Luke 1:5–20

A priest named Zechariah went to God's house to burn an incense offering. As soon as he was inside, the angel Gabriel appeared. "Zechariah, you and your wife, Elizabeth, will have a son. You will name him John," Gabriel said.

Zechariah didn't believe it was possible for Elizabeth and him to have a son. They were too old. "Because you don't believe me, Zechariah, you will not be able to talk until the baby is born," Gabriel said.

John was going to be a very important person. He would tell others to get ready because Jesus was coming.

A Baby Named John

Luke 1:57–66

Just as the angel Gabriel had said, a baby boy was born to Zechariah and his wife, Elizabeth.

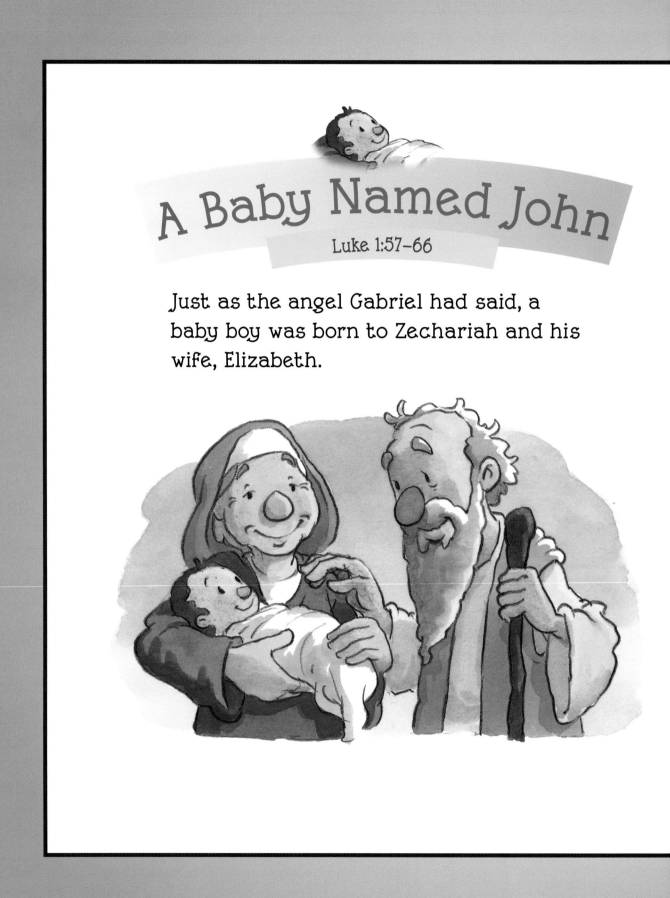

Their friends were very happy for them. "Name him Zechariah after his father," they said. Zechariah still couldn't talk, so he wrote down, "His name is John." As soon as Zechariah wrote that, he could talk again.

His name is John.

People don't get to see angels very often, but when they do, they need to pay attention. Angels bring messages from God. What is another way God sends messages?

Mary's Big Surprise

Luke 1:26–38

Not long after his visit to Zechariah, the angel Gabriel went to see a young woman named Mary. She was a cousin to Elizabeth, Zechariah's wife. Mary lived in Nazareth and was engaged to marry Joseph, the carpenter.

"Don't be afraid, Mary," the angel said. "God is pleased with you. You will have a baby and will name Him Jesus. He will be called the Son of God." This was a big surprise to Mary.

What would you do if an angel suddenly appeared right here in front of you?

Joseph Marries Mary

Matthew 1:18–25

When Joseph heard the news that Mary was going to have a baby, he didn't know what to think. He wasn't married to her yet. God loved Joseph and wanted him to understand that the baby was from God and everything was going to be all right.

So God sent an angel to talk to Joseph in a dream. This angel told Joseph, "Name the baby Jesus. He will save people from their sins." When Joseph heard God's plan, he married Mary.

The name *Jesus* means "savior." What does a savior do?

God's Baby Son

Luke 2:1–7

The ruler of the land, Augustus Caesar, made a new law to count all the people. Everyone had to register in their hometown. So Joseph and Mary went to their hometown, Bethlehem. The town was full of people. There was no place for Mary and Joseph to sleep.

Finally, Joseph found a place for them where the animals were kept. And that's where God's Baby Son was born. His first bed was on the hay in the box where the animals were fed.

Why do you think God would want His Son to be born where the animals were kept?

Some Sleepy Shepherds

Luke 2:8–12

That night, out in the fields, sleepy shepherds were taking care of their sheep. Suddenly an angel appeared in the sky. The angel's light was so bright, it hurt their eyes.

"Don't be afraid," the angel said. "I have good news for you. A baby was born in Bethlehem town tonight. He is your Savior. You will find Him lying in a feeding box."

Who was the first to hear about Baby Jesus?

What the Shepherds Saw

Luke 2:13–20

Then the whole sky filled up with so many angels no one could count them all. They sang, "Glory to God in heaven!" And then, when the song was over, the angels disappeared.

The shepherds hurried to Bethlehem. They found Mary and Joseph and saw Baby Jesus lying in the hay in the feeding box. The shepherds told them everything the angels had said about the child.

If you had been out there on the hill with the shepherds, what would you have been thinking when the angels left?

Gifts for Baby Jesus

Matthew 2:1–12

Soon many of the people who came to register in Bethlehem went home. Mary and Joseph moved into a house.

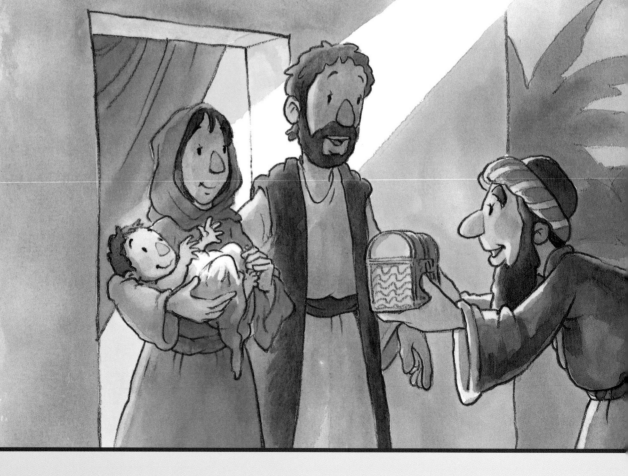

One day they had visitors who came from far away in the east. These visitors were wise men. They had followed a bright star to find little Jesus. They bowed down and worshiped God's only Son and gave Him expensive presents of gold, frankincense, and myrrh.

Why do you think the wise men came to see little Jesus?

The Man Who Ate Locusts

Matthew 3:1–13; Mark 1:4–9

Jesus' cousin, John, became a preacher when he grew up. He lived in the desert and wore rough clothes and ate locusts and honey. (Locusts were like grasshoppers.) John told the people to change their hearts and lives and ask forgiveness for their wrongs because Jesus was coming soon.

One day when Jesus was grown up, too, He came to the place where John was preaching and baptizing people. Jesus asked John to baptize Him in the river.

When Jesus asked John to baptize Him, do you think John did it?

John Baptizes Jesus

Matthew 3:13–17

At first John didn't want to baptize Jesus. He thought Jesus should be the one to baptize *him*. But when Jesus said it needed to be this way, John obeyed and took Jesus into the river and baptized Him.

As Jesus came up out of the water, God's Spirit, like a dove, came down to Him from heaven. God spoke and said, "This is My Son, and I love Him. I am very pleased with Him."

Jesus set a good example for us by following God's command to be baptized. Have you been baptized?

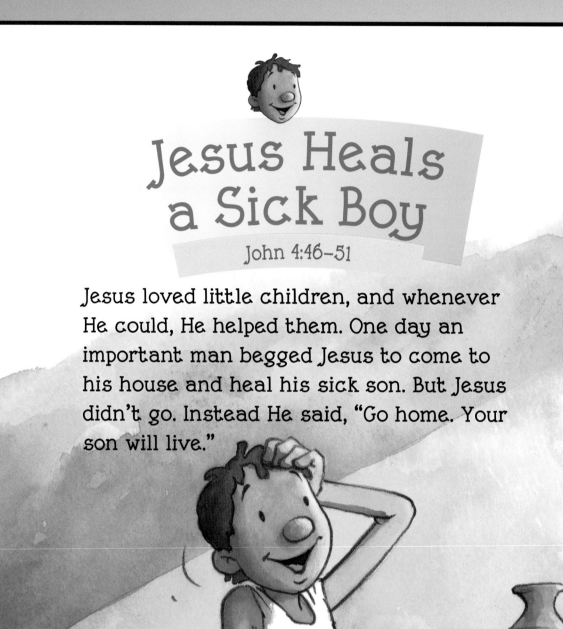

Jesus Heals a Sick Boy

John 4:46–51

Jesus loved little children, and whenever He could, He helped them. One day an important man begged Jesus to come to his house and heal his sick son. But Jesus didn't go. Instead He said, "Go home. Your son will live."

The man believed Jesus and went home, but before he got there, his servants met him and said, "Your son is well."

When we believe and trust someone to do something we cannot see, that is called *faith*. The man in this story trusted Jesus to keep a promise. Whom do you trust?

A Little Boy Helps Jesus

John 6:1–13

Great crowds of people followed Jesus
to see His miracles and hear Him teach
about God's love for them. The people
sometimes forgot to take food with
them. One day a huge crowd of 5,000 men
and their families followed Jesus. It was
late in the day when they reached Jesus,
and the people were getting hungry.

The only one with any food was a little boy with five small loaves of bread and two fish. Jesus blessed the food. His closest followers and helpers gave it to the people. After everyone had plenty to eat, the helpers gathered up 12 baskets of leftover food.

What do you have that you could give Jesus? An offering? Some time to help someone?

Jesus Stops a Storm

Mark 4:35–41

Jesus and His followers got into a boat and set out across the lake. Jesus was so tired that He fell asleep. Soon a strong wind began to blow. Waves came over the side of the boat. Everyone was very frightened.

They woke Jesus. "Help us, or we'll drown!" Jesus commanded the wind and waves to be still. The wind stopped, and there were no more waves coming into the boat. The lake became calm.

When you are frightened, what do you do? Remember, Jesus is always there with you. Just ask Him to help you. He will.

One Lost Sheep

Luke 15:3–7

Here is a story Jesus told. A man had 100 sheep, but he lost one. Now, what was he going to do? He left his 99 sheep safe at home and went looking for the one lost sheep.

He searched everywhere, and when he finally found the lost sheep, he was so happy. He put the sheep on his shoulders and carried it home.

How is Jesus like that shepherd looking for his one lost sheep? Remember, you are as important to Jesus as that one lost sheep was to the shepherd.

One Man Says Thank You

Luke 17:11–19

Ten men met Jesus as He was walking along a road. They didn't come close to Jesus because they had the horrible skin disease, leprosy. They called out, "Please help us!" Jesus told them they were healed and sent them on their way.

As the men went on their way, the leprosy disappeared. Only one man came back. He bowed down to Jesus and thanked Him for what He had done.

We should remember to say thank you for what God has done for us. What has God done for you?

The First Lord's Supper

Matthew 26:26–29; 1 Corinthians 11:23–25

While Jesus and His closest followers were eating the Passover dinner, Jesus took some bread and thanked God for it. He broke the bread apart and said, "Take this bread and eat it. Do this to remember Me."

Next He took a cup and said, "When you drink this juice of the grape, remember Me." Jesus knew this was His last meal with His followers because He was about to be killed. He wanted His followers to always remember Him.

Today in church we still eat bread and drink the juice of the grape to remember Jesus. We call this time of remembering *Communion* or *The Lord's Supper*.

Jesus Prays for Help

Matthew 26:36–40; Mark 14:32–42;
Luke 22:39–46

Jesus and His followers went straight
from dinner to a quiet garden. Jesus
wanted to pray and ask God to make
Him strong for what was about
to happen. He took three of
His closest followers—Peter,
James, and John—with him.
Jesus asked them to
wait and pray.

He went a little farther into the garden so that He could pray by Himself. It was very late, and the three men were very tired. They couldn't keep their eyes open to pray. Soon they were asleep. Jesus woke them twice, but they went back to sleep each time.

When we have tough things ahead of us, we need to pray and ask God to help us.

Jesus Is Arrested

Matthew 26:45–56; Luke 22:45–51; John 18:10–11

The third time Jesus woke His followers, He said, "We must go. Here comes the man who has turned against Me." Just then a big crowd carrying torches and clubs came into the garden. Judas, one of Jesus' followers, was with them. He kissed Jesus on the cheek. It was a signal to the guards to arrest Jesus.

Peter pulled out his sword and cut off
the ear of one guard. Jesus told Peter to
put the sword away. Then He healed the
guard's ear.

You might think the crowd would let Jesus go after
He healed the man's ear. Well, they didn't.
They arrested Him and took Him away.

Pilate Questions Jesus

Luke 22:52–23:25

Lots of people loved Jesus, but there were many who didn't like Him at all. After Jesus was captured in the garden, He was taken to the house of the high priest, then to Pilate, the Roman governor of Judea.

All night the rulers asked Jesus if He was God's Son. They did not believe that He was. Finally Pilate said that he didn't think Jesus was guilty. But the people who hated Jesus kept yelling until Pilate decided that Jesus had to die on a cross.

Jesus told everyone that He was God's Son, and that made some people very angry. But even if they didn't believe it, He was still God's Son.

Jesus Is Killed on a Cross

Matthew 27:27–40; Mark 15:25–27

Pilate's soldiers took Jesus and put a crown of thorns on His head and made fun of Him. Then they led Jesus out of the city to a place called Golgotha to be killed on a cross.

At nine o'clock in the morning, the soldiers nailed Jesus to the cross. They also put two robbers beside Jesus, one on the right and one on the left.

The day God's Son died on the cross was a sad day.
But God had a wonderful plan.
Keep reading and you'll see what it was.

A Dark Day

Matthew 27:45–54; Luke 23:44–49;
Hebrews 9

While Jesus was on the cross, the land became dark from noon until three o'clock. Then Jesus died, and there was a big earthquake.

When the earth shook, the thick curtain in the Temple between the Holy Place and the Most Holy Place ripped from top to bottom. Now people could see inside the Most Holy Place. Before, only the High Priest got to see inside. When the soldiers at the cross saw what happened when Jesus died, they knew He really was the Son of God!

Jesus died because He loved us. He died so that our sins could be forgiven. Let's tell Him right now that we love Him for what He did on the cross.

Jesus Is Laid in a Tomb

Luke 23:50–56

A rich man, named Joseph of Arimathea, had a new tomb where he had planned to be buried. He took Jesus' body from the cross and put it in his own empty tomb.

Joseph and Jesus' friends wrapped
His body in strips of linen and laid it
carefully in the tomb. Roman soldiers
came to guard the tomb. They rolled a
huge stone over the door and sealed
it in a way that would show if anyone
tried to move the stone.

Everyone thought that since Jesus was dead,
they would never see Him again.
They were in for a big surprise!

A Big Surprise

Matthew 28:1–10

The day after Jesus was buried was a holy day, so His friends had to stay home. Then very early on Sunday morning, the first day of the week, the women went back to the tomb. It was the third day since Jesus died.

When the women got there, they couldn't believe their eyes. The stone had been rolled away! An angel of God was sitting on the stone! The soldiers were so frightened they were like dead men.

How do you think those women at the tomb felt when they saw the angel?

Jesus Is Alive!

Matthew 28:5–8; Luke 24:9–12

The angel said, "Don't be afraid. Jesus is alive." Those women were as happy as they could be! They ran to find other friends of Jesus.

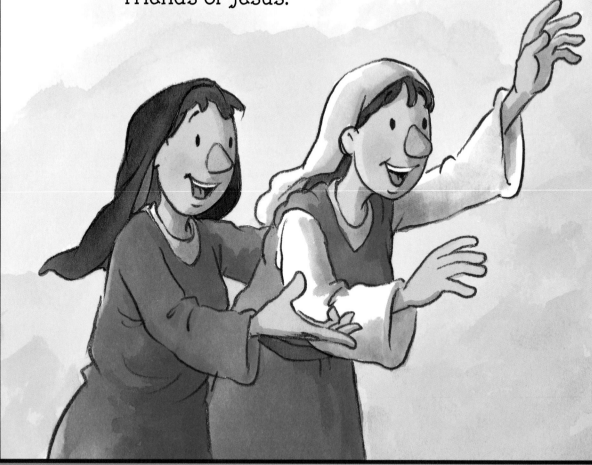

Some of Jesus' friends didn't believe what the women said. But everything the women said was true. Jesus was alive! He had risen from death.

How long is forever? Jesus promised He would come back to life . . . and He did. Jesus is alive today and will be forever.

Jesus Appears to a
Room Full of Friends

Luke 24:33–49

One night Jesus appeared in a room where many of His friends were gathered. He told them to tell their family and friends and neighbors and even strangers that He is alive.

He told them to share everything He had taught them. They were to tell the people in Jerusalem first, but then they were to tell people everywhere. Jesus told them to wait in Jerusalem until God sent them a special gift of power from heaven.

Whom do you know that would like to hear all about Jesus' love?

Jesus Goes to Heaven

Luke 24:50–53; Acts 1:6–11

Jesus led His followers a little way out of town. Jesus prayed for His followers, and while He was praying, He started to rise up into heaven. Then a cloud hid Him from His followers.

As everyone was standing there staring up into heaven, two angels appeared beside them and said, "Jesus has been taken away from you and into heaven. He will come back in the clouds, just like He went away."

Remember the gift that God was going to send? Keep reading and see what happened.

God's Spirit Comes to Help

Acts 2:1-4

After Jesus went back to heaven, His friends and helpers were praying together in a big room. Suddenly something amazing happened.

First it sounded as if a huge wind were blowing. Next flames of fire flickered over every person's head. Then God's Spirit came, and everyone began to speak in different languages. This was the gift from God that Jesus had promised His followers.

Jesus' friends were happy. God's Spirit had come to live with them and to help them.

Everyone Hears and Understands

Acts 2:5–42

The night that God's Spirit came to Jesus' followers, there were people from many countries in Jerusalem. These people spoke different languages.

When they heard Jesus' friends praying, they went to see what the noise was all about. They found Jesus' friends telling about the great things God had done.

But they were all surprised to hear it in their own language. "What does this mean?" they asked.

God's Holy Spirit still helps those who follow Jesus today.

A Mean Man

Acts 9:1–4

There was a mean man chasing after Jesus' followers. His name was Saul. He was sure that everything he heard about Jesus was wrong. He didn't believe any of it. He was sure he was right. So he hurt, and even killed, people who believed in Jesus.

Well, God wanted Saul to work for Him.
So one day when Saul was on a journey,
God sent a bright flash of light. It was
so bright, Saul fell to the ground.

**Why do you think God wanted
Saul to work for Him?**

Saul Is Blinded

Acts 9:4–9

"Saul! Why are you doing things against Me?" a voice said from inside the light. "Who are you?" asked Saul. "I am Jesus. Now get up and go into the city."

When Saul stood up, he was blind. His friends had to lead him into the city. Saul wouldn't eat or drink anything for three days.

**What will happen to poor, blind Saul?
Do you think he is ready to listen to God?**

Ananias Helps Saul

Acts 9:10–18; 13:9

God sent a man named Ananias to find Saul and pray for him so that Saul could see again. Ananias was scared of Saul. But Ananias believed in Jesus and went anyway.

Ananias prayed for Saul, and Saul's sight came back. On that day, God changed Saul's heart to make him kind to those who believed in Jesus. Saul was also called Paul. Soon Paul began to tell others about Jesus too.

Did you know that Paul became one of the greatest preachers who ever lived?

Earthquake!

Acts 16:16–36

Some people didn't like what Paul was preaching about Jesus. So they caught Paul and his helper, Silas, and threw them in jail. The two men were beaten, and their feet were fastened tightly so they couldn't run away. That night, instead of complaining or crying, Paul and Silas prayed and sang songs to God.

Suddenly there was an earthquake, and the jail doors popped open. The jailer thought his prisoners had escaped. He knew if the prisoners had escaped, he would be in big trouble. Paul called to him, "We are all here!" When the jailer came to them, he asked, "What must I do to be saved?" Paul told him all about Jesus.

If you had been beaten, thrown in jail, and had your feet pinned down, what would you be doing?

New Heaven and Earth

Revelation 21

One of the biggest promises God ever made was that we will live with Him in heaven forever. He said that there would be a new heaven and a new earth and we would get a new body—one that won't get old but will live forever.

In the new heaven, no one will ever be sad again. No one will ever die again. The streets will be made of gold, and there will be gates of pearl. Everything will be more beautiful than anything you can imagine. And best of all, Jesus will be there. We will be with Him forever.

What is the most beautiful thing you have ever seen? Heaven will be a thousand times more beautiful.

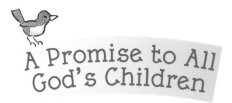

A Promise to All God's Children

"No one has ever seen this.
No one has ever heard about it.
No one has ever imagined
what God has prepared
for those who love him."

1 Corinthians 2:9